MW00900169

Kosmo's Christmas Delivery

Starring

Kosmo & Kramer

Written by Deb Kalmbach

Illustrated by Joey Palmberg

For Lucy & Henry

Deb Kalmbach always had a hunch her two Jack Russel Terriers, Kramer and Kosmo, could be stars in a children's book. The terriers are well-known in their tiny town in Washington State for creating chaos wherever they go! Even though *Kosmo's Christmas Delivery* is fictional, the story was inspired by Kosmo's real life adventures.

Joey Palmberg graduated in Fine Arts from North Park University in Chicago. He now lives in Washington and is pursuing all kinds of artistic projects, from comics and videos to his first children's book! He's really more of a cat person, though.

Kosmo's Chirstmas Delivery
Text Copyright © 2016 by Deb Kalmbach
Illustrations © 2016 by Joey Palmberg

Chiwalla Press 2016

They named him Kosmo. They should have called him Trouble – with a capital "T"! Don't ask me why they needed a puppy. They already had an exceptional dog – me, Kramer! But my family, especially Emily Jean, went all goo-goo-ga-ga over Kosmo.

"Oh, Kosmo, you are soooo cute!"
cooed Emily Jean.

"What about me?" I whimpered. "I was first."

Kosmo didn't have any manners.
He slurped his food *and* vanilla ice cream.
He licked his lips after nibbling corn-on-the-cob. *Smack! Smack!*

And potty training? Kosmo didn't have a clue.
"You're supposed to go outside!" I barked.

No matter what Kosmo did, Emily Jean
loved him all the more.

I was the Number One Dog.

Not anymore.

One day just before Christmas, Kosmo
and I snuggled in our beds dreaming
doggie dreams.

Suddenly, the Yellow Package delivery truck
drove into the neighbor's driveway.

Kosmo, King of Trouble, leapt up to take a look.
He watched the deliveryman, wearing a
Santa Claus hat, unloading packages.
Kosmo bolted to the door and whined.

"Good dog," said Emily Jean's mom.
"Thanks for telling me to let you outside."

"Good dog?" That's like calling a cat a smart animal !
Who's the *real* good dog?

Kosmo raced out the door. He ran straight
toward the Yellow Package delivery truck.

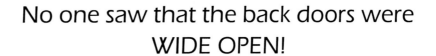

No one saw that the back doors were
WIDE OPEN!

"No, Kosmo!" I barked.
Wait... this might solve all my problems...

The deliveryman closed the doors
and climbed back into the truck.
He started the engine. And with that,
Kosmo and the truck drove away.

"Where's Kosmo?" Emily Jean asked
when she came home from school.
"Uh-oh!" said her mom.

I pretended I was asleep. Maybe if Kosmo never came
back, I would be the favorite dog again!

Emily Jean cried, "Kosmo is so little.
He's gonna be cold and hungry."

*He's a pest. I wish you never
got him,* I growled under my breath.
It's an early Christmas present.

Merry Christmas to me!

A teardrop streaked down
Emily Jean's cheek.
I didn't like to see her sad.
I ran to get my leash.

I guess we could look for Kosmo
...a little.

I dragged Emily Jean down the snowy sidewalks.
Maybe the Yellow Package delivery truck
dropped Kosmo off at Brady's Gas Station.
We always got treats there.

"Have you seen Kosmo?"
asked Emily Jean.
"Not today," Mr. Brady said, tossing me a treat.

What if the Yellow Package delivery truck
had taken Kosmo to an exotic,
far-away place like Fiji?

Kosmo could be sunbathing
on a beach, having the time of his life.

No fair!

Emily Jean tugged on my leash.
"Let's check the Duck Brand Diner."

I rolled my eyes.
Kosmo had visited there *once*.
A waitress had almost dropped a tray piled
high with dishes when Kosmo raced past her.

"No sign of Kosmo today," sighed the relieved waitress.

"Remember when Kosmo escaped from the car and ran into the grocery store?" Emily Jean asked, looking hopeful.

How could I forget? Several customers and a bag boy chased Kosmo down Aisle 5. They finally caught him next to the broccoli. But no one had seen Kosmo today.

Even worse, what if Kosmo got sent to the dog pound?
I felt something hurt inside me.

Emily Jean asked everyone about Kosmo...
everyone except Mr.Tramble.
No one in the neighborhood liked Mr. Tramble.
He kept his curtains closed.
I heard he kidnapped dogs.

We both shivered as we hurried past him on our way home.

I curled up alone in my bed by the fireplace.
The flames crackled and danced.
I should have felt happy. Something was wrong.

I missed Kosmo. Yes, I did.
He was my friend – even if he was a troublemaker.
I looked out the window. Christmas lights sparkled.
Big, fat snowflakes swirled down.

Please come home, Kosmo!

I woke up early the next morning. I yawned. I stretched.
No troublesome terrier attacked me while I tried to sleep late.
Yes, I was the favorite dog. No, I didn't
feel one bit good about it.

I peered out the window, hoping to see Kosmo trotting
toward the house. Instead, the fur stood up on my neck.
My nose told me danger. A huge man lumbered toward the
house carrying a box. Mr. Tramble? Oh, no!

Emily Jean's dad opened the door.
"Good morning, Mr. Tramble."

"I don't see anything good about it. This package
came yesterday and the box is damaged! It's my
Christmas fruitcake. Well, it *was* my fruitcake.
It's half-eaten," Mr. Tramble grumbled.

I couldn't stop barking.
There was more than fruitcake in that box!

Mr. Tramble opened the box. Curled up, covered in
fruitcake crumbs, was a little ball of white fur.

"Kosmo!" I yelped.

"Kosmo!" Emily Jean squealed.
"Kosmo?" her parents looked
at each other in disbelief.

Emily Jean scooped Kosmo out of the box, crumbs and all.
He wiggled into Emily Jean's arms.

"Oh thank you, Mr. Tramble. Can we get you another fruitcake? " Emily Jean's mom smiled.

"No, thank *you*. I'm glad someone *else* ate it!" Mr. Tramble said with a big toothy grin.

Kosmo, who was worn out by his travels,
snoozed in his bed.

I snuggled next to him.

I had gotten the best present of all,
Kosmo was home.

Merry Christmas to me!

Made in the USA
San Bernardino, CA
04 November 2016